FATAL APPROACH

Their Gaze, Her Love and the First Lady

Martha Stewart

TABLE OF CONTENTS

THE CELEBRATION

Eighty-six thousand, six hundred and twenty-one dollars.

The end result is equal to the money we raised that night. We had driven through the county and north across the state border, collecting green garbage bags with the bills locked up in self-storage facilities. The sacks were usually wrapped in an old, tattered paint sheet or hidden between similar sacks filled with used clothing of scrap dealer quality. The collected sacks filled both trunks of large American cars when it was over.

We had taken two vehicles with us - one following the other close enough to offer protection, but far enough away not to be detected. I drove with my friend Ronnie. He was the only one who knew where we were going until we got there. Both cars were equipped with handguns for each man and also a sawn-off shotgun for each man in the back seat - one in each car. It was the first time I had seen Ronnie or any of his guys with loaded guns.

It was so scary I almost peed my pants, but I wanted to be more a part of Ronnie's world, and Ronnie's world was dangerous and illegal. It was a surreal experience from start to finish. That special kick you get when you know you shouldn't do something but feel so cool that you wouldn't miss it for the world.

I didn't know whether the weapons were to protect us from a possible robbery by rival groups or from a shoot-out in case of a police intervention. I didn't want to think about what could have happened either way.

Eighty-five thousand is probably not a lot of money by today's standards, but back then it was enough to buy a very nice house even in big cities. It was more money that I thought I would ever see in one go.

That was real drug money. It was not like in the movies with crisp hundred-dollar bills nicely stacked in a leather briefcase. The bills were wrinkled and torn from the time spent in blue jeans bags - enough to get a horny boy and his girlfriend high on Friday night. A teenager was given $5 to go to the roller rink, instead they were spent to buy a few loose joints. $20 that a fast-food worker made and used to buy a gram of crank. The change from a couple of trips to the store for the mother never returned to her and instead bought some black beauties.

These were street drug money, collected over time by some of Ronnie's local distributors. It was a bunch of it. Not a single $50 bill in the stack and very few of them. It was currently lying on my bedroom floor, stacked in stacks of $100 so we could count it all.

Ronnie and I had counted and recounted the money for hours - we stopped at regular intervals to laugh, drink, draw a line and fuck occasionally. It's a pretty hackneyed scene from a B-movie these days to see a drug dealer and his girlfriend rolling around on a bed of money, but we did it loud and proud, as if we'd invented the idea. Ronnie was pretty high from his nightly score, I could see that, and he rode me pretty hard, which I had no complaints about. The sex was electrifying and fun and became more and more inventive the further we went.

It was damn hot, and I enjoyed it so much that I couldn't think straight, and I let him throw me around on the bed so he could take me the way he wanted. I wanted him to take me and make me cum all over the money, even though some of the bills smelled pretty disgusting.

I was just a little uncomfortable because I knew that four of Ronnie's friends were in the house - all wired, buzzing and armed to the teeth. The creaking bed and the unsuppressed moans and giggles were nothing they hadn't heard before, but I tried not to think about it. (It's hard to have too much privacy when you live with a drug dealer).

Every time we finished fooling around, we had to count the stacks that we hadn't tied with rubber bands yet. I sat there naked and counted some of the money, which was maybe the third time, while Ronnie admired the view. Every now and then he'd break another piece of coke or roll up another joint, and if I was embarrassed, I'd beg him to stop.

After a while Ronnie realized that it had been a while since he had looked after his boys - and with over $80,000 in the house I could tell we were a bit paranoid, even though we were having a good time. He put his pants back on and left the bedroom to check in.

I heard them talking - and again reminded myself that they could hear us too - and heard one of the boys ask Ronnie "when it was their turn". It was Mark, a big bully of a man who had been driving all night with a shotgun in the back seat of the second car.

There was no humor in his voice. That wasn't Mark just bullying Ronnie. Suddenly everyone became calm, and even from the other room I felt a certain tension. It was a problem every time a bunch of drugged up gangsters got into an argument, but for me it was twice as important, because Ronnie was the only one in the bunch who wasn't heavily armed.

After a much too long silence, Ronnie murmured: "Dude, you haven't been here long, so I'm going to excuse you this time. She is different and she is mine... "You want some pussy, we'll get you some, but let's put the fucking booty away first."

I could tell by the footsteps that Ronnie had walked away from the door after he said this - his attempt to move the conversation away from the bedroom door and my ears. Mark didn't seem happy with the answer. He muttered, "It doesn't seem right - you're having all the fun while we're sitting out here with our tails in our hands. As time went by I would find this man more and more unpleasant.

When Ronnie came back into the room, he had a couple of big old suitcases with hard side walls in which we had piled $70,000 of the money. $5,000 he stuck to the bottom of drawers he'd taken out of my bedroom dresser and nightstand. Another $8,000 he sat aside to pay the boys - he slipped this into a brown lunch bag and dropped it next to the door.

Then he turned off the light and I suspected that this meant it was time for sleep, which was a good thing, since it was perhaps 4:00 in the morning. But Ronnie wasn't finished yet, and as soon as he was lying naked in bed he manoeuvred my head down and I knew exactly what he wanted me to do. While I was serving him, he gave me instructions - Ronnie never did that before. I knew he was mocking Mark.

That kind of theatricality was just part of living with Ronnie, and I had learned to find the humor and even the power in it. But this time I became restless and I tried to withdraw and tell him to stop. He had none.

He had his hands firmly on the back of my head and I could not stop until he had finished. Ronnie almost never came in my mouth, even when I wanted him to, so I knew that this was 100% for show. He knew that Mark was probably sitting outside the door. That was Ronnie - he let people know who was in charge. I could say that it made me feel cheap - but the truth is I kind of liked the feeling that I was special enough to cause friction.

When he finished, we finally fell asleep, but around 8:30 he woke me up to give me some instructions, saying he had to go away for a while.

He told me to take his $5,000 out of the dresser over the next few days, $500 each in 10 different checking accounts we had set up around the country. Ronnie also let me know that the $621 that wasn't in the thousands piles was mine.

I knew that the other guys had been promised $2000 each for night work - but I didn't feel cheated at all. I was just a feast for the eyes - not an armed bodyguard - and would probably have gone for nothing.

Finally he told me to put my hair up, put on some make-up, then put on the nightgown behind the door and make breakfast for the boys. He and I both knew that wearing this thing was so thin that it was almost like being naked, and that was the point.

I never met Ronnie at moments like this. I did what I was told - I understood my hair and my morning swollen face as best I could. I bent over to put on some panties, but Ronnie stopped me, shoved my ass and basically threw me out of the room.

The moment I hit the hallway, four pairs of eyes were hit by the body and remained there. The gown hung on me like wet paint, and I was painfully aware of this. Although all the shades in the house were closed because we were not afraid of prying eyes, enough sunlight still came in so that they could capture my silhouette through the thin fabric.

I continued to make breakfast, flinching inside whenever I had to bend down to get a pan or open the refrigerator with its bright interior light. Ronnie was right behind me on the way out of the bedroom, so at least I knew everyone would behave - and they did - and thanked me for breakfast and even picked up their pies and put them in the sink when they were done - which they certainly didn't do at home.

Breakfast was served, Ronnie and the crew quickly packed up, and I didn't see or hear from them for almost a week. (I was worried all the time, too - I didn't even trust Ronnie's people when I knew there was $70,000 available there that they could consider their own and make with a few shots).

When I did, it was as if our lives suddenly shifted into a whole new gear. That $70,000 was used to buy us into a whole new business with higher stakes and higher payouts. I didn't know it at the time, but Ronnie had bought an area and sold his soul to a so-called cartel. They were less violent back then, but they were still people you don't know that well.

Before it was over, I would get too involved in all this, but I was young, naive, and all I knew was that we seemed ten feet tall and bulletproof. We had money, powder and power.

Until we didn't have it anymore.

THE LINE

It results from "should not" and "must not". "I can't, I don't want to". Please don't do this to me. It's a lie because every muscle in my body wants to touch me and my skin is burning to taste.

I'm going to say that he's my opposite and everything I shouldn't want and can't have. I can stand in front of him and just the sight of him makes the blood rush through me and make me throbbing. And I have no fucking idea why. But I do, of course I do. He's rough and stocky, and if I met him, I'd bounce off him. He's curvy and he's heavy and everything about him is bigger and stronger and uglier. He's my opposite, and I want him to defile my femininity. But he must not. I won't let him, because I belong with my husband.

But what if I were to...?

What if I didn't look away when I feel his eyes moving over my body? What if I leaned over the desk and allowed him a closer look at the cleavage, which I know he has spent many nights thinking about fucking. What if I whispered into his ear all the dirty things he does to me at night when I think about him.

It would be so easy to touch his chest while I do it that he would wonder if I had lost my mind or if he had finally broken my resolve. I wouldn't tell too soon - I would play flirtatiously, whisper a little "No, I can't" as he went in to kiss me.

He'd run his lips over mine as I pulled away. I can smell him; the oil of the machines he works with, the tingling of the new sweat, his breath and his body. I want the smell of him to stick to me as if he was marking me. He can see the conflict in my eyes.

I can't. I must not. But haven't I crossed the line already? Our lips met, so if I'm doomed to guilt, I should eat my fill.

In a split second of weakness, I press my lips to his. I feel the roughness of his beard, and his tongue feels strange as it enters my mouth. I am not used to being kissed like that by anyone else. I shouldn't do that. But as I cross that line, I realize again that I'm already ruined. All I can think about is the feeling of his big, rough fingers inside me.

I love that, and I'll tell him that. Nothing can save me now, because he hastily slides his hand under my skirt and I open my legs to give him access, as if I give in to his will or resign myself to it. My thoughts stray to the fact that we could be caught and there would be no covering up. Here I am, legs spread, sitting on his lap while he pushes my soaked underwear aside and the tips of his rough thick fingers probe the pink creases of my cunt. I feel ambushed as he sinks his fingers inside me, as if he is taking my second virginity. My innocence is gone; I am a fraud. It is beyond ecstasy. He knows what he is doing while waggling his fingers inside me. The pressure on my G-spot makes me squirm and whimper like a frightened animal out of control. I have spent so many nights thinking about this.

I see that his face is consumed with lust and I realize that although he is honestly excited to finger fuck me, I really want to give something back. His cock is hard through his pants, and if there is one thing I have thought about more than him finger-fucking me, it is the thought of blowing him. On my knees at his whim; the ultimate submission.

I already know he loves that. I figured it out from the subtle things he said and the way he looked at my lips. I remember once, at his request, I guiltily sent him a photo of my face. His joy at such an inexplicable image made me think...

So I kneel down, unzip and reveal the cock I had imagined for as long as I could stretch out every fuckhole I could offer. I want to show him what I can do. I spent years honing that skill on my husband. His cock is humble, and I'm grateful for that because it's easier to handle. I start with his balls, enjoy the taste he has and that unmistakable masculine smell. I like to lick and suck gently while giving a show of myself, making occasional eye contact with him. The insolence of my eye contact underlines my fall from grace. I want to be his bitch.

I lick and kiss the veins of his shaft. I look at the head of his cock glistening before coming. I like to play with him as if he were a lipstick by pulling the tip of his cock over my open lips. I can taste him. It is salty and warm and I enjoy it as if it were a delicacy. I know he's watching me, so I make sure he sees me willingly humiliating myself and my morals.

I suck gently at the tip, using mainly my lips and guiding it with my hand in my mouth. He's getting more and more urgent, so I allow him to fuck my mouth. The feeling he has in my mouth is satisfyingly uncomfortable. It's almost a sadomasochistic kick that I get. The elation brings my mind to bliss. I'm wet and throbbing between my legs. I want him to lick and fuck me until orgasm, but when his dick head presses into the back of my throat, it brings my orgasm mentally closer. I try to open my throat for him, but it makes me choke. He ignores this and I enjoy the kick that comes with it, disregarding my right to comfort.

My orgasm becomes more pronounced, and I doubt it takes much to push me over the edge. When he starts masturbating on my face, I rub myself and bring the orgasm to a ticklish climax where "before" meets "after" and "I must not" becomes "I did it". This rush to my head makes my muscles weaken and for those few seconds I ride my orgasm and nothing else exists anymore. My body contracts rhythmically and I scream. I feel his sperm hitting my skin, first hot and then quickly cooling off.

And then it dawns on me - I am a cheater and he has made me his little whore.

THE CEOS WIFE

A colleague of mine was a strange guy with a lot of strange stories from the old days in the steel mill. He had even published a book about life in the steelworks, mostly a book with lots of black and white pictures.

One day we visited a plumbing shop. Some students had a great idea, probably trying to be funny, so they poured cement into the sink on Friday afternoon, and of course the sink had to be replaced.

We went over to the desk to place an order. Behind the desk sat a nice woman in her early fifties. Pretty fit and hot. I could well imagine that she was very hot ten years ago.

Back in the car my colleague was laughing. He said he had seen how I looked at her as if I was a dog and she was a bitch in heat. He laughed at his own remark.

He told me that she was married to the big boss, the CEO, as they call it today, of the old steelworks. The plant where I used to work. She divorced him, five guys, myself included, got fired. I looked at him, he smiled. We fucked her, the big boss found the proof, she divorced him and we got fired.

I looked at him and I laughed. Without saying a word, he started the car and we drove back to our school and the cemented sink.

The next day after lunch he showed me a thick envelope. His hand moved it across the table towards me. He blinked.

I opened it and found a photo album. On the front was a big yellow flashing smiley face. He said these were the unpublished pictures of life in the steel mill.

Page one, a picture of her... a black and white picture. She was dressed nice and neat. Classic skirt and blouse. Just like a secretary. She was hot, she had a beautiful smile, and she had this thing. I find it hard to describe, some women have "sex" written all over them.

He told me that in her younger days she was, and still is, the hottest girl in town. Of course she married the big man at the mill. Rich, big house, but a really boring economist. His humour was as dry as the Sahara, and he could drive a person crazy with boredom after a five minute conversation. But he was good at running the mill.

His wife worked as a coordinator at the mill, booking meetings, fixing conference rooms and so on. She was the opposite of her husband. She flirted, laughed, was happy and sexy.

I turned to the next page in the album. Next picture, also black and white. Her in the middle, light-gray skirt, short tight, white blouse. And two dirty guys in helmets, coveralls and safety shoes. She was laughing, her whole face was laughing.

He went on talking while I looked at the picture, describing how things developed over the years. How her little flirt with the boys evolved from little hints and blinks to more boldness, and how the boys' comments evolved from little comments about her beauty to more direct comments about her body.

Again I opened a new page. In this picture she was standing in front of a desk, leaning forward and holding a pen in her hand. A normal position in an office. Except that her head was turned back and she was smiling, she looked directly into the camera and blinked.

When I looked at the pictures, my colleague told me that he had a good relationship with her. How he was a talented photographer back then and how she enjoyed his attention with the camera and that all the pictures were taken with her permission.

I turned to the next page, I was quite excited. On this page there were two pictures. She was in a mechanical workshop. On the first picture she held a grease gun in one of her hands. She had a devilish smile and a spoonful of grease in the other hand. On the other picture she sent the photographer a teasing smile as she rubbed the grease with her fingers.

When I looked at the pictures, he explained to me how things had developed over the years. How her flirting had become rougher and rougher and how the boys, like in these pictures, introduced her to different things in the workshop. Like the grease gun. How they told her that day before the picture was taken that the fat was Vaseline. And how they responded to her more direct flirting, she responded to her sexual attention. A mutual pleasure is the right words.

I turned to a new page and was curious about the next picture. It was in a break room where the boys were eating their lunch. She was sitting at the table with the boys. I noticed that it was the same boys in all the pictures. Four boys and the photographer. She was holding a banana in her hand and the tip in her mouth.

My assistant continued the conversation, but I didn't listen much.

I quickly turned to a new page. I'm not sure what I expected, but I was not disappointed. There were four pictures, artistic style, and like all pictures in black and white. No colours. The first picture, a dark room, the flash of the camera made her white shirt look very white, a dirty industrial worker hands her the tit. She smiled and looked into the camera. Second picture, another hand on the other tit. Other hand, bigger. Third picture, both hands removed, but her white shirt was not so white anymore. Two dirty handprints on her tits. In the fourth picture, a guy kissed her neck and three others stroked her.

The contrast between her beautiful white and grey clothes and her dirty hands and overalls was fantastic.

My colleague said that this was her game, she was in full control and then he left the room.

I stared at the pictures. I remembered the nice woman in the plumber's workshop. Her smile, nice and polite.

Again I looked at the fourth picture. Her eyes were closed, she leaned with her back against the man who was kissing her neck. Her face was turned upwards towards the ceiling. Her mouth was half open.

On the next page, a picture, it was the workshop. A dirty mattress on the floor. She was on her knees. Still dressed, but not as clean. Four guys around her. She smiled into the camera.

I turned the page. Almost the same picture, but all four had erect penises, and she was holding two in her hand and sucking on one. She wasn't looking into the camera right now.

On the next page, the fourth guy was sitting behind her. He had pulled her skirt up around her waist. His hand was between her legs from behind.

New picture, close to her face. A cock in her mouth, eyes half open, animal lust. The angle of the photo was good, and I could see the fourth guy smiling, and I imagined his fingers deep in her holes.

I closed my eyes. My dick was rock hard. These pictures were much better than a modern digital HD home train.

I flipped to a new page. She was standing, skirt around the waist, shirt around the waist. A hand pulled up her black panties, they were enclosed by her pussy panties. Some other hands pulled her tits and squeezed her nipples.

One hand pulled her head back after her hair, and a finger was in her mouth. I imagined a hard time for her.

In the next picture, scissors cut off her panties and bra. Skirt and shirt still around her waist. She was still held by many hands and because of the view of her nipples they were not tender. She looked down. Whether she was looking at the scissors, the nipples or at what I could not make out. But one thing I could say. She was horny. Her eyes and her mouth could not lie.

I looked at the picture for a long time. Every detail. Her white skin had traces of her dirty hands. Tits red stains from pinching.

My hand turned to a new page. It was lifted by three men. One on each side and one holding her head. It was nice to see how they treated her with care and not at the same time. The fourth man sat between her legs. The face was buried in her crotch. Her nipples were stiff, and the expression on her face made her groan.

New page, new picture. Her pussy, close up. She was glistening. Swollen pussy lips, a swollen clitoris. A dark, hairy finger stuck halfway inside her. Or it was on its way out. glistening from her white, creamy juices.

Next page. She was still held between the fingers. She pulled her hair, raised her head up and looked down herself. The fourth guy was between her legs. He showed her the grease gun and a big grease spot, or Vaseline, on his finger.

I quickly turned to the next page. A picture from a good angle. It shows a knuckle deep in the butt and face. I couldn't remember ever seeing a woman with a hornier expression on her face.

From here it was a series of pictures of her basically getting fucked in every direction, in every hole. They changed positions here, on all fours, on her stomach, riding, on her back. Fucked in the pussy, fucked in the ass, fucked in the mouth, DPed. Certainly sucking the cock that had fucked her in the ass. And cumshots in pussy, ass and mouth. And a really red ass with a distinct handprint.

The last picture was of her lying on the mattress. Exhausted. She was glistening with sweat, semen and salvia. Smiling in a tired, happy way.

I closed the album. Surely I would never be as horny as I am now.

My co-worker entered the room. He smiled. She told me that somehow her husband found out about it, and that was the end of the marriage and our work. These pictures are the only copies, and you're the only one who saw them.

Maybe we should go to the store and visit her one day. He winked at me and smiled.

NEW OFFICE

Despite the various restrictions imposed by the corona virus, I was able to start my new job on Monday, and it had been a hell of a week. I had just finished my last scheduled session on Friday and was thinking about lunch when my phone rang.

"Amy!" I answered happily. "What are you up to?"

"Well, it's been a long time since we've had lunch, and I was curious if you'd like to eat," she said.

"Sure. Where are you?"

"I'm down in your building. After you told me the good news, I thought I'd come out and surprise you."

"Fantastic. I'll be right down," I said, hanging up, grabbing my coat from the back of the door, then walking through the empty office space to the elevator.

I got off the elevator and saw Amy. She was wearing leggings and a sweatshirt with a zipper. Based on past experiences, I could clearly remember the busty figure she was hiding under her humble clothes. Despite the social distance, I gave her a big hug and felt her face and chest pressing against my torso.

"It's good to see you! You look fantastic, as always," I said.

"Thank you," she blushed slightly. "You look good too. All dressed up like a boss," she said, flicking her tie.

"You know me, I'd rather be in a T-shirt and cargo pants. But you gotta do what you gotta do, right? Besides, Lisa likes it," I said in allusion to my wife.

"I bet she does," she said as we headed for the parking garage.

"Where are the children?"

"At home with Sean. I said I needed a ride after being cooped up for so long."

I opened the door for her, and then I put myself in the driver's seat. My dick twitched, remembering the times we fucked in the same car over the years.

We swung by a local gyroscopic joint and we were able to drive off, because all the seats were closed. Since we had nowhere else to go, I suggested we eat in my office. Amy agreed it was the only option that made sense.

We laughed as we remembered it and caught up. Most of our interactions in those days took place through social media where we checked each other out.

"Nice office," she said, looking out of the floor at the windows on the ceiling as I pulled a chair up to the desk and cleared some space for us to eat.

"Yes," I smiled proudly, "it's all right."

We sat and ate and laughed, and the stress of the week disappeared from our minds. Our knees shook a few times, and when she leaned over to steal one of my fries, I stole a peek into her shirt to get a glimpse of her ample cleavage.

Once, when she bent down to speak, her hand rested on my thigh just above my knee.

When we finished eating, I leaned back and said, "What a pity we didn't get dessert.

"Maybe we can think of something else," she said, moving her face closer to mine and turning her chair towards me.

"Perhaps..." I leaned towards her repeatedly in silence, my hands sliding up her thighs to her hips and then to her waist.

She wrapped her arms around my neck and our lips met.

I had neglected to kiss Amy. She was such a passionate lover, and it makes cheating, which was true for both of us at the time, even hotter.

Without breaking the kiss, I took one hand and pushed the leftovers of lunch onto the desk, then grabbed them by the hips, picked them up and lifted them up to put them on the desk.

She giggled playfully and pulled me towards her while I pressed my body against her.

To waste no time, I kissed down her neck and my hands moved up her chest, over her sweatshirt that covered her voluptuous bosom. She moaned as I touched her, expressing the same lust that had swollen inside me.

I leaned back and pulled the zipper of her shirt down, revealing her tits covered with a black bra.

"That's so hot, baby," I said and bent over to kiss her cleavage while I held her tits in my hands.

She took off her jacket behind her and then felt her bra loosen as she must have opened it from behind. I let it fall from my hands as I kissed up to one nipple, sucked and nibbled at her and then went to the other, her fingers running through my hair.

I withdrew to kiss her again, our mouths opened, our tongues danced. My hands pulled my tie apart when I felt her hands finding my belt. As I unbuttoned my shirt I felt my zipper come down and then my boxers were pulled down so she could grab my stiff cock.

She stroked me before pushing me back and slipping from the desk to the floor. When she started kissing and licking my naked cock, I took off my shirts and threw them on the floor with the growing pile of clothes.

I moaned loudly as she began to take me in her mouth. My hands rested in her hair and held it out of the way as she started to bob.

"I missed your mouth," I said, my eyes closed and my head tilted back as she teetered and sucked and licked me.

There was a popping sound as she pulled her head off my cock.

"I missed sucking you," she said, and then went back to him.

As much as I wanted her to go on for hours, I knew our time was running out, so I pulled her up and turned her over to the desk. I grabbed her leggings and panties and pulled her down by her shapely legs while she looked at me hungrily over her shoulder.

I laid my cock at the entrance of her already soaked pussy and pressed my head inside. Amy moaned loudly as she laid her head on the desk.

I slowly rocked into her, enjoying the feeling of her pussy, which was intensified by the sound of her squeaking and moaning. In a short time I was deeply buried with my balls and enjoyed a pussy I had not had for years.

"Baby, you feel so good," I said as I picked up speed.

"Moooooorrrreee", she moaned as she came on my cock.

I pulled it out, turned it around, put it on the desk and dived back into it.

Her tits bounced and giggled on her chest as I stomped off.

"Sperm, please," she moaned. "I need it in me."

The feeling was so incredible I wanted to fuck her against the window, but I couldn't deny her what she wanted.

"Ahhhhh," I moaned loudly as I came in her spurt after spurt, my hands holding her hips.

"My God", I said, my head tilted back, my cock still stuck in her pussy.

"I missed you," she said, "but I really missed that."

I pulled back and sat in the chair.

"Do you want to clean me up?" I asked with a grin.

Moaning, she fell back on her knees in front of me and took my soft cock in her mouth, sucked it carefully and licked it clean.

"I wanted to fuck you against the mirror."

"I wanted that too," Amy replied. "Maybe next lunch," she said before putting me back in her mouth.

NEW CAR

Jasmine and I left the restaurant laughing.

Jasmine: I have a new car.

Me: You got rid of the Subaru?

Jasmine held up the keys: Yes, since my mother-in-law lives with us and romps around with the kids, I needed something bigger. It's a Volvo. It's nice.

Me: Better than the Subaru?

Jasmine, laugh: I hated the Subaru.

Me, reaching for the keys: Let me see.

She gives them to me as we walk over. I unlock and look inside: Spacious. You could take a nap in here. (We laugh.) How does she handle it?

With Jasmine: She's fine. I like her.

Me: Can I take it for a quick spin?

Jasmin: Jasmin: Do you have time?

Me, looking at my watch and smiling: It will be alright.

Jasmine: It will be all right.

I climb into the driver's seat while Jasmine gets in on the passenger side. I take the opportunity to look at her legs and feel myself getting stiff.

I start the car and put the SUV in reverse. The Volvo drives gently out of the curve. I start the car and leave the parking lot.

Me: That's nice. How much is it?

Jasmine: 43

Me: Not bad.

I'm walking straight down the street where our old office used to be.

Me: You rented out the old room. It's now the headquarters of some bank.

Jasmine: Cool.

Me: There's our old place. Should I stop over there?

Jasmine: You are so bad.

Me: Well, you were wearing a dress...

I put my hand on her thigh and press her hem slightly upwards.

Jasmine: I was wondering when you were going to say something about that.

Her eye blinks as her mischievous grin grows.

I turn into the parking lot where we park after work and walk towards the shady spot.

Jasmine: I can't. You have to go to work and I have to go home.

Me: Just for a minute?

Jasmine (grinning and biting her lip): Just for one minute?

I'll park the car and leave it running.

Me: (winking): Yeah, just for a minute.

I lean forward as she leans in, our lips kiss. No sooner was the contact established than she grabs me and pulls me towards her. My hand continues to slide up her thigh and my other hand grabs her hip. She pushes herself towards me and pulls me closer to her over the centre console.

I (breaks our kiss): Let's see how big her back is.

Jasmine, her breath ripping, moans approvingly and climbs over the centre console and into my back. I take off my suit jacket and climb back following her.

Without any loss of time she immediately climbs onto my lap and kisses me. My hands grab her ass and pull her further on me. Her double-Ds are pressed against me.

My dick is pressed against my pants.

My hands move up her sides and find their way to her chest. She moans into my mouth.

Jasmine: I dream of it.

Me: Me too.

One of my hands is rubbing her nipple through her dress, while the other is returning to her thigh and pushing her dress up on the way to her panties.

She's rubbing up against me.

Me: You're rubbing my pants.

Jasmine: I'm sorry, Jasmine. (She continues to crunch.)

Me: Let me help.

I kiss her deep and then move her from my lap. I reach down to loosen my belt, but she is already grabbing my zipper. As I undo my button, she reaches into my boxers and grabs my cock.

Jasmine: I missed that...

She starts to caress me.

I pull down my pants and she lets go of me for a moment. As soon as my pants are down, I lean back and she bends over to suck me into her mouth.

Me, by my moaning: I missed your mouth.

My left hand rests on her head as she bounces and sucks while my right hand reaches around to caress her chest.

Without removing her mouth, she climbs up and puts her knees on the seat. My right hand pulls up her dress and I put my hand on her panty-covered ass and squeeze her.

Me: This is so good...

I pull down her panties on her thighs and put my hand on her dripping pussy.

She's shaking and pulling her mouth away from me to moan.

Me: Come here.

I pull her up and kiss her. She slides closer to me.

Me: Climb up.

I: Jasmine: Please...

She sits on me and lowers herself down on my cock. My hands are on her hips under her dress, while I make sure she doesn't go too fast and enjoys every inch as she slides down.

Jasmine (begging): Please...

I pull her down and fill her up.

Jasmine: Thank you. I needed this so much.

She swayed her hips as she snuggled against me.

Jasmine: So good, so good...

Me: You feel incredible.

I push into her while she rocks against me. I hear her breathing faster and then she hums.

Her body trembles as she pauses for a moment while I am buried deep inside her.

Jasmin: That was amazing!

Me: More?

Jasmine: Jasmine: You cannot come inside me.

Me: Okay.

I turn us around and lay her down and climb on her. I hammer my only regret into her that we don't have time to take off her dress and let me fuck her tits.

Jasmine, moans quickly as she builds to another climax. She shudders at me again as I look further inside her.

Me: I'm going to cum. Where to?

Jasmine: In my mouth.

She presses herself against me and while I lean back, she climbs back on her knees and lifts her butt up into the air. She devours me while I put my finger in her dripping pussy.

As she keeps sucking and bobbing, I push myself up to meet her here. My hands move to the back of her head and help to guide her in an original way.

Me: Here I come.

My back arches and she intensifies her sucking while my tail stutters. She continues sucking until I lean back and take my hands off her head. She swallows my semen while I breathe.

Jasmine: I have to go now.

Me, looking at my watch: I have to go too.

We adjust ourselves and climb forward again.

I, while we are retreating, put my hand on her thigh: That was great. Thank you.

Jasmin: Thank you. I needed that so much.

Me: So, can you have lunch again next week?

Jasmine, grinning: Maybe.

BED REVIEW

I took a photo of the pendant on the bed and sent it to you with the message: "Your wife said she loves my bed".

You would understand it as the picking up boys do to each other all the time, if you would just perceive it in such a way that I am referring to the time when she had slept there, when she lived with her sister and we were all out and about, or when you both had slept there while you were babysitting for my wife and me. You have no idea that we had collapsed in a pile of wrapped limbs on top of each other after we'd been fucking hard for a morning or an afternoon.

But we hadn't just shagged in my bed. We used every opportunity to steal a quick fuck. We'd done it once, when we went to get everyone coffee. And every time we had lunch together, now that our offices were within walking distance, we'd wet my cock. Your bed was best when you were downstairs with her family and we had put our respective children to sleep.

Sometimes these were quick naps where I would take him deep and fast and leave her with a pussy full of cum. Another time we took our time and I enjoyed every inch of her petite body.

And I know you don't make her blow you because she thinks it's not right for a man and a woman to do it, but I do. We're already doing so much wrong that I make her suck my dick like she's drowning and it's full of air. She's a natural. I took it from her bubbly personality that she'll be a donor, and I've not been disappointed.

And these secrets we share, like the fact that you cheated on her once in the lounge or the secret trips to the strip club? Well, she knows, and let me tell you, kid, she fucks well when she wants revenge.

She wanted to confront you, but I knew a better way for her to get back at you, and that clearly had something to do with her setting me up. But I couldn't just tell her that. I had to convince her myself.

So over several days, over lunch and text messages, I led her down a trail of crumbs. We talked about how you were the only man she'd been with, and that you were probably who you always were, and that you wouldn't change. We talked about the effects of divorce on the children and how upset her parents would be. We talked about how she was just trying to get over it, and that no matter how much time passed, every time she looked at you, she would still see your infidelity. We talked about revenge, but how nothing she did to you would ever equal that.

That's when I told her it was really about how she felt. If she agreed to get over it, it would only affect her, just like if she didn't. So I told her to do what would make her feel better, even if she was the only one who knew.

At the end of this lunch she gave me a big, tight hug, the first time she really pressed her body against me and let me feel her breasts bouncing against me. She thanked me and we planned to have lunch tomorrow.

The next day she seemed nervous and a little awkward. At first she said that everything was fine, but when I pushed her, she finally decided that she had decided what to do, but she needed my help. I told her that I would do whatever I had to do because I just wanted her to be happy.

She kept telling me that she had never been with anyone else but you and that she had never seen anyone else, she hesitated to see her naked before. She decided that she wanted to take revenge, even if you never knew, because it was about how she felt about it, as I had said. So she looked at her phone and then back at me and told me she was ready.

My phone beeped, and I noticed that I received a series of messages. When I looked, I saw that they were pictures of her from her bathroom at home. As I flipped through the pictures, she had less and less to see in each one, so she absorbed the digital striptease she was playing to me.

I let my excitement and attraction show on my face when I finally looked at her nude photo. I tried to burn every inch of her sexy body into my memory, from her shaved hill to her sassy tits to her aroused nipples. I was careful to bite my lip when I looked up from my phone. As I looked up from my phone, my eyes slowly moved up her body, clearly undressing her before me.

She was crimson, and I knew that in this situation I had to strengthen her self-confidence. I began by telling her how beautiful she was, how amazing her body was and how amazingly brave she was to take this step. I laid my hand on hers when I told her how much it meant to me that she trusted me and decided that I could be trusted too.

She relaxed and held my hand and thanked me again for all the help I gave her and my support. We ended the lunch with many flirtatious looks from her and I made it clear that I was taking a close look at her. After we finished our lunch, I took her back to her office as usual, only that I took every opportunity to finally check her out openly.

The next day we met again and again for lunch, and again and again she sent me a set of pictures, this time in sexy lingerie, with her undressing. The next day it was the same and this time in different underwear. And every day more cleavage was shown, so that I could see with my own two eyes what I could only see on pictures before. Every day I made sure that I let her know how beautiful and brave she was.

On Friday, after another series of lingerie strip photos and a flirtatious lunch, she took me back to her office by a different route. When we arrived at a place where nobody was around, she hugged me again and then leaned over for a kiss. That was our first kiss, deep and passionate, and I finally had the opportunity to grab her ass and squeeze it while we kissed.

When my wife and I came to your house this weekend, we both pretended that nothing was going on and nobody seemed to notice, especially you.

On Monday at lunch she took me to her car instead of our regular place. As soon as we entered the elevator of the parking garage, I couldn't help but wrap my arms around her. We kissed angrily, both of us persisting in our hunger and passion for the other. Only when the elevator door closed after we reached our floor did we stop our kiss, although no one got out. We pressed the button to go back, but it was too late, our elevator had been called to another floor. We did our best not to laugh so much when the other person got in and the three of us returned to their floor.

After we got off, she led us to her cabin, stealing an occasional kiss and I grabbed her waist or butt. When we arrived at the car, I lifted her onto the hood, wrapped her in my arms and made out with her, pulling me against her with her legs and arms, hitting me with as much of her body as possible.

She broke our embrace and told me we should get in the car. I gladly did her the favor of letting her climb into the back seat and pat her butt as she continued to crawl in front of me. I climbed in and sat down next to her but before I even sat down we were hugged again. My hands were finally really free to stroke her body.

My hands found a way under her shirts, touched her naked skin for the first time and I could hear her breathing. I pushed my hands up, felt her flat stomach and rubbed her back. We had leaned closer together, practically over each other.

I pulled her onto my lap, and because of her petite size she had some headroom. My hard cock was now pressed against her pussy, closer than ever, despite our pants and underwear. I twitched it against her and heard her moaning again.

I pulled her shirts up and she forced me to let her take them off. I took a moment to feast on her white bra-clad breast before kissing, licking and massaging her. You are a lucky man.

She undid her bra and dropped it when she bumped into me. She must have been so aroused because it only took a few minutes before she played with her tits, kissed and crunched them. It was a pleasant surprise, especially how overwhelmed she seemed by the experience. Later I learned from her that this was her first orgasm. Of course it was not her last.

After she had come, she insisted on taking care of me as well, so she slipped off my lap and sat down next to me. I let her unduly drop my pants and helped her to let them slide down. I was rock hard and she couldn't help mentioning that I was taller than you.

She started to caress me and when I encouraged her to take it in her mouth, she apologized that she was no good because she only did it a few times. It's really your loss.

I've had girls in the past who were never that good, and here she rocks my world. And to top it off, when I blew my load, she didn't even pause. She swallowed that shit. I complimented her on her skill, which made her blush. It was just the first of many blowjobs she gave me, either as her main event or as a prelude.

We finally did it a few days later. We both called in sick and got a hotel room instead. She really dressed up for the event, with her make-up and lingerie, a new set she had bought just for me.

I fucked here in every position imaginable, which was an experience for her, considering she told me that you only do a few punches and a grunt. She loves to drive, which works well, considering how many times we've done it in cars.

She also loves the puppy, which also worked to our advantage, because she is adventurous and has the potential to get caught in public. We have banged in parks, parking garages, family bathrooms and even a few times in the woods. The craziest ones were of course in one of our houses, in the middle of the night, when we sneak into the kitchen or living room and do a quickie.

Anyway, that first day really set the bar. I must have injected into her five or six times, and one of them was in her mouth. I remember that because she came when I came in her mouth. Unbelievable.

We only snuck away a couple of times for a whole day, I'd like to do more, but we only have so much time. And I think we should do it soon, considering you've been talking about having another baby. While it's exciting to think about getting her pregnant, I'm sure that everyone would realize that it's my child.

Anyway, I look forward to fucking her in your new bed.

THE NEW ADMIN

WOW a new girl in the office. I am speechless.

"Hello" is all I can do with a little smile.

Man, it's hot in here, it must be me. She is hot. Slim, petite, with a nice smile. Small, perfect tits, hot legs. Uhhhhh... what did I come here for? Oh right, I need to speak to your boss. With one last smile on the new girl and she goes back to the shop to fix more equipment. The rest of the day I'm locked in a daydream dreaming about seducing this beautiful woman, but I noticed a ring. I'm not a cheater, but damn it, I could cheat with her!

My daydream is a distraction because it goes on every time I see her. The seduction would be so sweet. For the past few days, I can't even remember her name. Her boss is an ass and doesn't formally introduce new employees. Finally I find out that her name is Nat. Natalie.

The daydream grows more vivid as we talk over the next few weeks. I wonder if she caught me staring at her in a daze. Hey, pumpkin, get a grip. You don't have a chance, you're both involved with other people. Days go by, but my imagination of her seduction doesn't fade. I learn more about her and her life. She may not seem like a cheating girl, but a boy can dream.

It would begin at a place we both agreed upon...

Hot kisses and caresses. I lead her into the shower, our hands gliding over each other's bodies as I sensually pull off her skirt and low-cut blouse while the hot water in the bathroom rises steaming. I fiddle with my clothes while she undresses them hungrily. I turn her around and bring my hands around her neck to her shoulders and down the sides to her hips and pull her close to me. She raises her arms and wraps her hands around my head and neck. I kiss her just below the ear and pull kisses down to the shoulders while taking the bra strap first from one shoulder and then from the other. I put my hands around her sides and clasp her beautiful breasts tightly. She pants and emits a small groan while I pull her towards me and pinch her neck together. She lowers her hands to my sides and pulls my hips closer to my hips, rubbing her butt against my erection. Now it's my turn to moan.

One sharp inhale: "Natalie."

"Mmm, I like the way you say my name. You make it sound so sexy. Say it again."

And then a muffled whisper. Natalie.

She turns to me without breaking off contact. I brush her hair back and wrap my fingers around her with one hand, the other holding her tight little back against me. I lead her face upwards, exposing her neck, leaning in for a kiss just below her jawbone and moving slowly towards her collarbone. I bite gently while opening her bra and throwing it to the side.

We move into the waiting hot water and let it pour over us. She puts her hands around my head and pulls me to her chest to get the attention I need. Slowly I lick her nipple and take it in my mouth. Natalie moans a little and I feel her tremble. I move to the other nipple and she trembles again, pressing my mouth even harder into her breast.

"You're driving me crazy," she moans.

"Well, you've been driving me crazy for weeks, and now I finally have you. I guess a little payback is in order."

I start hauling kisses into her navel. Natalie writhes and lets out a little giggle. She pulls me back to eye level to show me the desire in her eyes. We pour the hot water over each other as we explore each other with our hands. I grab some soap and quickly lather up something to make us nice and slippery. I press her against the shower wall and attack her neck again. She lifts her leg around my hip to drag her smooth hill against my throbbing cock. The feeling she has against me is electric and I am ready to come from the heat of our passion to orgasm. I need more. My desire to hear this beautiful woman in orgasm is overwhelming. I pull her tightly against me and start kissing and licking me to her navy as I pour the hot water over us. I put her leg over my shoulder and get a first glimpse of her most private area. I put a kiss just over her hill and slowly pull my lips towards her beautiful clitoris. I split her swollen lips to expose her clitoris. She pants and pushes her fingers into my hair and leads me to where she needs more attention. I lick her clitoris and close my lips around the delicious little bud and suck gently.

"AHHHH Fuck". No more quips. I want you."

"Not yet." I tell her while I slip two fingers inside her pussy and roll her up to rub her G-spot.

"Ahh." She gasps. "I need to feel you."

"MMM. "No, I want you to come for me first." As I continue to rub her G-spot and put my mouth back on her clit and twirl my tongue around and start sucking on that delicious little nub.

"Please!" She's begging me. "I'll be right there."

I look up at her with a smile. "Come for me, Natalie. I want you to come just for me."

I come back to lick her nectar. Her body cramps as her pussy squeezes my fingers and I feel a warm flood wash into my waiting mouth.

"MMMMMM FUCK, I want you so much," she screams.

She pulls my hair and tears me from the beautiful pussy that gave me pleasure. She lifts me up until our eyes meet.

"Take me to bed" while she wraps both legs around my waist and her arms around my neck and holds me tight. She pulls my head back and nibbles my neck, and the electricity of her touch weakens my knees as I fiddle with the shower door to carry her to the waiting bed. I sit her down on the corner and gently lay her feet on the floor. She loosens her grip, but tries to pull me close to her.

I tear myself away from the hot kisses she demands and slide down her hot body, kisses after, until I stare at her beautiful pussy again. I put her hot little feet on my shoulders and expose her all over me. I kiss the tender spot where her thigh meets her body.

Natalie moans." God, you make me so aroused. I want your cock inside me. I need you now."

"I'm sorry, Natalie. I want to see you cum. I want to taste your sweet nectar when you come for me.

"Mmm, I like the way you say my name. That is so sexy. I don't usually use my full name, but it gives me goose bumps when you say it."

"Mmmm... Natalie."

I moan in her beautiful pussy and slide my tongue from her entrance to the top of her hill. She breathes in small breaths through clenched teeth as I use my fingers to spread the hood around her swollen clit and wrap my mouth around it. I nibble at her, taking care not to bite too hard. Her fingers are intertwined in the sheets as she screams

"Ahh FUCK... Enough!"

She pushes me away with her feet until I'm on the ground, and then she slams on top of me and pushes me down. She pulls my nails into my chest as she spreads my hips.

"Now it's my turn to tease her." She tells me so, a smile on her face, her eyes burning with desire.

She slides her fingernails across my chest and then down my arms. Our fingers entwine as she scratches her pussy on my cock. She glides along without allowing me to reach her entrance. Her touch is electric as I feel the heat of her gorgeous pussy almost making me let go.

"Ahh... Natalie, you're making me cum."

A wicked grin spreads across her beautiful face.

"Not so funny when we tease, is it? Now it's my turn to get what I want."

Natalie rolls her hips and bends over to guide my cock into her pussy. She slowly descends on me. Now it's my turn to gasp and shake.

"Oh my God, you're so perfect." I moan. "Tease me. Please me. Use me. Use me."

She leans over and bites my earlobe.

"I need you deep inside me. I want to feel you coming."

Natalie starts rubbing up against me and I can feel her cervix pressing against the tip of my dick.

"Ahh... you're so deep. I want you so much."

She moves forward until only the tip of my dick is left in her, then she pushes her pussy back and pushes our pubes together. The pace accelerates with long, full blows. Our breathing comes panting and moaning as our hunger increases. I adapt to her blows. She digs her nails into my chest.

The excitement with which she takes control is electric as I place my hands on her breasts to gently press her nipples between my fingers and apply pressure until she moans. She slides her hands up my chest and bends forward, crossing her arms behind my head and holding my hands on her nipples. I lift my hips according to her strokes and let the pressure build. I can feel her excitement. The pressure is almost unbearable.

"Mmm. Natalie, I'll be right there."

"Oh, yeah... come inside me. I want to cum with you. I wanna feel you.

I push hard in her pussy and I rub my cock deep, my pubic bone against hers. I can feel her pussy tightening and I'm swaying my hips.

"Oh YES", she screams.

I can't hold myself back any longer because this familiar rush goes right through me.

"Ahh Natalie." I scream as I try to pull her hips even closer to mine.

She makes a deep groan and trembles as I let go deep inside her. She leans back and digs her fingers into my hair and pulls my head against her breasts. I move my hands to bite her nipple and she screams as her pussy contracts and milk every drop of me.

We break down with her on my writhing chest and let her hair fall around us and wrap ourselves in a hot, sweaty cocoon.

"Wow," she says and whispers hoarsely, "How about an encore?"

CHEATING YOUNG GIRLFRIEND

Ever since we met in college, I've been warning myself about what other people would say about my girlfriend. As a nineteen-year-old sophomore, Annabelle was the girl who seemed innocent until you met her. I had known her since the late freshman year of high school and had witnessed her blossoming within two or three years from a clumsy young petite blonde with no sexual experience to an extremely sexually mature young petite blonde.

When I started courting Annabelle in my last year of school, she was a virgin with little appetite for sex. After I had seen her for about two years, she had transformed into an unprecedented level of sexual appetite and fervour. As a strapping, young, petite blonde, Annabelle had limited herself, and I knew it. My craving for porn and erotic stories finally made me succumb and attracted her. At first it started quite innocently, with my own subconscious urging us to play different scenarios. We started with the most obvious scenarios, such as the messenger and the bored housewife. After some basic nudges, Annabelle started to enter these role-plays each time with an extremely wet center. I started testing her sexual boundaries with my hands and fist until I could no longer nudge her with my fingers or penis alone. However, her favorite role-playing game took place towards the end of her climax and involved a hypothetical large penis penetrating her and killing her.

On a whim, I used a debit card that my grandmother had given me for Christmas to buy a toy for Annabelle and me to play with as we rang in the New Year. My mistake was ordering her toy while I blacked out drunk at a Christmas party. The party had caused me to miss the 22nd with Annabelle and my family. Annabelle added to my frustration by sending me a picture of her in red underwear and matching bra, fucking the fake Christmas tree we bought. When I looked at this photo and drank a bottle of liquor at my desk, I suddenly had a tendency to order sexual toys. A few clicks further on I realized that her "present" had no chance to arrive until Christmas and still ordered the most realistic but inconspicuous dildo I could find in a drunken stupor. In my drunken state I thought I had ordered a soft looking pink dildo that Annabelle could play with in front of me.

Instead I had somehow ordered a realistic black cyberskin dildo. Amazon only made me aware of the difference in memory when the package arrived. Ashamed, I checked my phone on Christmas Eve and saw the recent delivery. I checked my drunk purchase and was ashamed. Hoping to return it, I created a return option since I had finished work for the day. Without my knowledge at the time, my girlfriend had knocked on the door half-naked and signed for the box. Without thinking, my girlfriend took the box into her bedroom and opened it, thinking the contents were a BLU Ray or Xbox controller. Instead, the plastic lining of the cyberskin dildos revealed itself, and without thinking, she tore open the box. With little interest, but much remorseful horniness, Annabelle spent the next few hours exploring the inside of the packaging on her own. Towards the end of the working day I checked my account again and saw that the package had been delivered. I clicked on the product details and saw first hand my drunken mistake. The sexual toy I had ordered for my young girlfriend and me to experiment with was 9" long and simulated the size of a real BBC. I checked the shipping details and was shocked to learn that it had been updated to show that it had been delivered to the front door.

Instead of dealing head-on with the impending "delivery", I let the problem resolve itself naturally. Without the actual dildo product, I naturally assumed that the "misdirected" toy had been delivered to the wrong address, and I continued with my normal life when I received my credit note in early

January. During a fairly routine dive into the issues of the year, I saw the delivery of the toy. As Annabelle went into the store, I rummaged through the walk-in closet, expecting to find nothing but curiosity. After looking around briefly, I found the black cyberskin dildo. I suspected it had been lost, but inspected it more deeply, found it smelling of sexual fluids and stowed it away.

I decided to ignore the find and let the toy walk around the bedroom apparently without my knowledge. This went on for 2-3 months until my girlfriend used my laptop for a project and forgot to log off. Not only did she forget to log out of the course website, but Annabelle also forgot to log out of her Apple ID and the media and the following photos were synchronized. Knowing that the deadline was tight, I searched her computer while she was using the toilet. In just a few minutes I had logged into her website and checked the results. Not only did Annabelle have an Adult Friend Finder account that filled automatically, but several other dating sites showed up. Curiously, I checked each address in her browsing history and loaded the associated websites.

Nineteen-year-old Annabelle not only had pictures sent to her by other people, but she also had sexually suggestive pictures on each of the profiles I flipped through. Strangely enough, my penis hardened when I looked through my girlfriend's robust search history and remained erect the whole time. Never before had I been fascinated by the thought that my girlfriend's vagina had been "misplaced" and enjoyed by someone else. But the thought crossed my mind as I poked around on my laptop. Finally I could no longer hold the thought back when I found the 9 inch cyberskin dildo in Annabelle's panty drawer. I got into the panty drawer almost immediately. I came almost immediately after discovering it, but hid it from myself. I now saw the length and circumference that only a toy of this size could have. I continued to place the big dildo in the usual place and was amazed every time I could secretly pick it up and insert it into Annabelle while we were having normal sex.

Almost three months after Griffin began to notice that Annabelle was coming home with an increasingly less tight interior, he became surprisingly wise. And yet, as the relationship between Annabelle and Griffin changed, no one spoke directly about the difference. That is, until the discovery that would change their deep and painstakingly managed relationship forever. One afternoon, I came back early and parked my car in the driveway. I walked from the garage into the living room and heard the unmistakable sound of moaning. Instead of feeling my blood boiling and my face glowing red all by itself, I held on to that feeling and continued to listen to the muffled moaning and screaming.

Instead of attacking the source of the animal noises I stood in the entrance and listened apparently forever.

Finally I was overwhelmed by the source of the noises and I crept quietly up to the master bedroom. When I reached the top of the stairs, I was struck by the depth and extent of the infidelity that was occurring at that moment. My typically shy girlfriend was lying splayed on my desk when a tall black gentleman stood between her legs and kept pushing forward.

I watched in shock as every second at least seven centimetres of hard black penis rammed into my young white girlfriend. I could see Annabelle's face from my vantage point and it was clear that she was contributing to most of the satisfying sounds. Instead of interrupting the action, I hid and tugged at my penis when my little friend finally came and pulled out the black cock and shot across Annabelle's face and mouth for almost a full minute. Watching the thick ropes of cum cloud my sweet girlfriend's face proved to be too much for me, and I soon lost my short blows. In no time at all I was left standing onmy side while my girlfriend went to a restaurant to eat with the big black man while she was covered with his sperm and did not respond to my own text messages.

ETERNITY IN A MOMENT

Alli chatted with Nick for a few weeks. They had had a social conversation the Sunday before, and she was a little surprised that she wanted to meet him. More surprised that after seeing her, he seemed more attracted to her than ever. She had called him "Sir" a few times and knew that he loved that - he called her "Kitten" by now - partly because her screen name contained "Cat", but also because of the Snapchat filter photos she had sent him, which always had cat ears on them.

She had been reading his stories for weeks and was so incredibly turned on by them - now she was just turned on talking to him and had found herself incredibly horny after their conversation on Sunday. They were both married but frustrated - she thought she was practically a virgin - she had only ever been with her husband, had only ever felt touched by one person and longed to explore. He was naughty, perverse and had an evil side that excited her.

In the beginning she had only chatted and sent stories and occasionally a teasing photo that she had sent him. But lately she had found out that he had given her some orders and she enjoyed obeying him. Then he had asked for a hug and told her how much he had longed to kiss her. She was conflicted - she had never cheated on him, but with Nick she was tempted and excited. They were in the same boat, eyes open and not out to fall in love - just explore some naughty fun together. She decided to meet him for a talk and a hug and see how things went. They had agreed that if she called him sir while she was with him, he could kiss her.

The morning of the meeting dawned bright and clear - she was curled up in bed when Sir's "good morning" message arrived. He again said cheeky and nice things that made her smile, then he sent a photo of "what she had done to him". Fucking - his dick looked thick... she felt the wetness start between her legs, announcing the need to be fucked. She flirted a little, then finally got up and moved. He sent her some stories to start her day off. She hurried around knowing that she had to leave soon, half of her clothes were packed when she suddenly noticed that she didn't wear panties - it wouldn't be the first time she went without, so she put on the pink bra she liked, her black dress and leggings and headed off to work.

The next few hours seemed to drag on, she felt horny and nervous and insecure at the same time. Both were working, so there was little news. She tried to concentrate on her work, but was distracted again and again as she checked her phone, remembered the look on his tail, how wicked his imagination was and wondered how far she was ready to go this afternoon. Lunch arrived and they talked, he sent more stories she hadn't read just yet - she was horny enough already. But his words calmed her down - she knew he wouldn't pressure her, so she was looking forward to seeing him. She mentioned the missing panties to him, and his predictable reaction almost made her giggle.

Back to work for another hour or two, and then it was time. She made her way downstairs - full of doubts and some nagging insecurities - did he really like her as much as he said? Could she go through with it? When she came home from work, he told her where to go and she walked around the building to the little side street where she could see his car. Slowly she walked to the car and remained determined as she reached the car, opened the door and slipped in next to him. He smiled cheerfully and greeted her cheerfully with the words she learned to love... "Hello, kittens."

Hello", she managed to get out - she felt the nerves and horniness fighting inside her - he asked her if she wanted a hug and she decided that this was exactly what she needed at that moment. She leaned over to him and felt his arms hug her. She was protective and at the same time comforting and arousing. She began to relax a little. She smiled at his remark that she smelled good. His fingers caressed her arm and back through the material of her top. She wasn't sure, but she thought she felt him almost kissing her crown and then pulling back. They talked briefly about their work and the chaos there after some outside visitors. Then he asked about the stories - she explained that she hadn't read any of today's yet, and he suggested - quite firmly - that she read one of them now.

She felt her shyness pressing to the fore, but decided to obey him. She turned away so that she would not look at him while reading, opened one of his stories on the phone and started reading. As she did so, she felt his fingers gently on her neck - stroking in slow, gentle circles. When he asked her if it was okay, she sighed in agreement - it felt good on her neck after the stress and chaos of the last few days - but it distracted her and didn't help her horniness at all. She started to read and felt that the low throbbing excitement turned into a fire. She squeezed her legs together and wondered if he had noticed her deeper breathing and the changes she was trying to mask as she felt the need burning inside her. She wanted to kiss him. Shit - she wanted to do more than kiss him, but would she be able to handle it afterwards?

She decided not to read the second story just then - she couldn't really concentrate on it anyway. She slipped into his arms, rolled against him while he held her - the two thoughts arguing back and forth in her head. His soft words in her ear reassured her that there was no pressure, that they could just do what they were doing and that he would be happy. He could be, but would she be? The conversation revolved around his stories and the

adjustment he had made to the previous meeting - where he had turned a friendly encounter into something evil, and she had loved it. He whispered softly in her ear what he would write about today's meeting, and she moaned softly - the fantasy sounded so good - but would reality be any better?

He asked if she was really not wearing panties, and with a cheeky grin she pulled down the edge of her leggings to show her bare hips and waist. This time it was his turn to moan - the word "fuck" slipped gently from between his lips. When she said she was also wearing the pink bra she knew he loved the photo, and he said, "Prove it," she smiled with a slightly cheeky grin and pulled her dress all the way up to show the gorgeous bra and breasts she knew he loved.

Now she could see the lust burning in his eyes and she was so aroused. They talked - cautiously above expectations - it wasn't about love or about hurting anyone - it was two people who were inquiring and trying to do it in a safe way. She looked at him, his eyes, his smile, the gentle firmness with which he had encouraged her, while at the same time taking care not to be pushed or pressured. "Yes, sir..." she whispered. His arms slid around her and his lips met hers. She was soft, searching... the first time she had kissed anyone but her husband. It tasted different, but good. Her lips met and explored, his hand slipped over her soft skin - it felt like an eternity to her, but there was no dramatic outcry in her head. Just the desire to go on - to explore more.

Nick slowly pulled away and smiled at her - she knew how much he wanted it. His gentle words telling her she was a great kisser made her smile. He bent over again and she kissed him eagerly once more. They stayed like that for a while - ignoring the two or three cars that passed them. This time, when he broke the kiss, he undoubtedly knew how to turn her on. His soft voice reminded her that she had to be back at work soon. Then he asked a question she didn't dare answer.

"Is there anything else you'd like me to do before you leave Kitten?"

Fuuuuuck... there was so much she wished for - but she shouldn't go so quickly - should she? In a deep and shy voice she asked him to play with her breasts.

His hand quickly slipped up her dress and lifted it. His deft hands scooped her breast from the cup of the bra - his fingers teasing and pinching her nipples. Her need was now almost too great. She did not think beyond how amazing it felt. Then she felt his fingers caressing her legg-covered pussy and his apology. She didn't want his apology - she wanted his fingers. He had said he wouldn't go that far today, but she needed him to do it, and the way her body reacted to him, she knew he knew it too. So when his whispered voice asked him if she wanted his fingers on her clitoris, she answered immediately with the "Yes Sir", which she knew he would like to hear.

They were with her in a moment, slipped between her soaking wet pussy and found her clitoris in seconds. He knew what he was doing and in a few moments she had her first orgasm. She came, on the fingers of another man, in his car, in the middle of the day in a side street in the city. That was the naughtiest thing she had done in her life. She exploded to a second orgasm. She could have squirted further and further, but Nick suddenly pointed out the time - he didn't want her to get into trouble - and if she was any later, she would be. He pulled his fingers back and held her gently in his arms as she came down. She couldn't believe what she had done, but she didn't regret it. It had been amazing - and she felt that it was only the beginning.

CARRYING ANOTHER MANS SEED

It starts in my bedroom. It's a weekday morning and you've been there for two hours. You've already come inside me twice.

Now you sit on the edge of the bed and I kneel between your legs and I use my mouth and tongue for your cock, balls, stains and asshole.

For 20 minutes now I've been using my tongue and mouth to make your semi hard cock hard enough so you can try again to get what's left in your balls into my pussy. I'm starting to feel your frustration with my inability to get you hard again by seeing how you started grabbing my head and saying the things you started to say. You're also deeply frustrated that I'm not carrying your baby yet.

We were screwing for about 10 weeks at this point. We managed to meet a few times at my apartment, one night at a hotel and surprisingly many times in bathrooms and changing rooms. All together you managed to come inside me over 30 times, but it didn't work out.

The situation has worsened as we have moved forward. Originally, we both injected so violently within minutes, but given the sheer amount of sex in such a short time and the danger and risk, we both really increased what we were both willing to do.

Even this morning, when I opened the door, instead of telling me something, you just grabbed me, squeezed me over the back of my couch and stuck your cock inside me. I had learned by then not to bother me with underwear because it would just get torn off my body, or with your frustration when I wasn't wearing a dress or skirt in those bathrooms. You come into me quickly and roughly from behind.

Your cock continues to pulsate and you push deeper into me to make sure that you fill me as much as possible. You have wrapped my hair around your fist and still haven't let go.

Finally you pull back and tell me to get ready for the next round. Put on the white underwear and white stockings and prepare myself for a time that will not come easily.

In the last weeks the physicality of our relationship has really started to intensify. It took more than a month, but you have finally found and exceeded my limits and boundaries. The first time you managed to do this was in our night at the W-Hotel in the city centre, where you brought me to the ground by the combination of belt and riding whip and I said our safe word.

You were very happy at that moment and quickly climbed up and got inside me while I was lying helplessly on the bed. Your only concern that night was that my screams before you gagged me would cause someone to call the reception or that the marks you left on my body would arouse suspicion in my husband.

Today it would be no different, and after you had roughly taken off your underwear and left only your stockings, you tied me to the bed face down with my bottom in the air. At first you slowly use the leather whip we bought weeks ago on my ass, pussy and legs. You can still see some of your semen when it comes out of my insides.

In the beginning I only move my body away from the whip, but in the end, when I break and can't anymore, you use all your power on me.

This time there is no gag and you are happy about my squeaking and screaming. Of course, that made you rock hard, and you quickly mount me from behind. My moaning and pleading for you to put a baby in me makes you even harder. You tell me that you make me "scream louder now than in 9 months when the baby suckles". You stop deep down inside when your whole weight is on me.

It takes you a few minutes to recover and remove your now soft cock from my pussy filled with semen. You look down at your handiwork and see your sperm coming out of my pussy and the welts you left on my ass and legs. You think maybe you went too far this time, because these wounds are slow to heal.

This concern doesn't last too long and you tell me that if my body would only carry your child, you wouldn't have to fuck me so much. That once my belly starts to swell and my breasts fill with milk, you probably wouldn't have to use the belt and whip to get hard anymore.

You spend some time catching up on work, but you won't let me take a shower because you think you might give me a charge before you have to leave. You tell me to get between your legs and make you hard again.

Since you are still not quite hard and time is running out, I tell you to do whatever you need to do to get there.

You pull me up by my hair and hit me hard in the face out of frustration, the sound of the slap and the shock in my face seem to excite you. Four more times you bring your hand back and the slaps sound. This has had the desired effect on you and you throw me on the bed.

You hold my legs against your shoulders and kick me, push your now hard cock into my wet pussy ... My stocking-clad legs are pushed further back while you try to fuck your cock even deeper into me ... You squeeze the soles of my feet together and work on getting my feet almost completely behind my head ...

Almost completely bent in half, you have full control over my body and I feel you coming closer as you start to move faster. You start to give me some really dirty names and suddenly you punch me in the face for more time and tell me to tell you what you need to hear. I'm asking you to stick your semen inside me, fuck a baby in my stomach.

When you come closer, you put a hand around my neck and start pressing while your orgasm builds up. I feel you start to let go inside me while you call me a dirty cunt and your baby factory. Your hand tightens at my throat as you shoot into me and I get reckless and start to see stars. Finally you stop humming inside me and let your hand out of my throat.

Finally you pull your cock out of my pussy and hold my legs up to make sure your sperm stays in it. You tell me you're not sure what else you can do to put a baby inside me, but you emptied everything you have into me.

You take a shower to get back to your office... You come back into the room in a towel, staring at my body, and even though you have nothing left, you still want to fuck me.

You take out your phone and start taking some photos and videos and move my body into the positions that show your cum inside me or the marks you left on my body.

You grab my chin and kiss me passionately and deeply while your hand gently caresses my belly, hoping that this time it finally worked.

FUCKING THE FIANCÉE

It was well after midnight, and Leo was in a great mood. It was the first night of an amazing festival, and he had stayed out late to watch the last set. Now he wandered back to his tent and the rest of his friends in tears, slightly confused by the flag system, but sure that he would arrive eventually.

As he stopped to fill his bottle from the petrol pump, a small, incredibly drunk guy staggered towards him.

"Yoodude, whatsupp!! He slipped, his arm drifted up and hit his fist.

'Hey man', Leo replied. "I'm a bit lost!

'Ohh, that's, uh,' the guy opened his mouth unsteadily and staggered to the ground. Reflexively, Leo caught him before he struck. Then the guy threw up. Most of it missed, but some of it dripped onto the guy's shirt.

Damn it, Leo thought.

"Sorry, sorry," mumbled the drunk.

"Come on, man, where are you? I'll get you back', Leo said resignedly. He wasn't the most caring, but leaving this guy lying in barf just didn't sit right.

After a few minutes of slow stumbling they reached one of the smaller tents. The man had fallen into a kind of dizziness, but when he saw that the tent brought some energy, he came back to himself.

Katie, hey! Katie!," he groaned as he crawled unsuccessfully for the zipper of the tent. There was a pause, and it was reversed from the inside out.

Ricky', cried a girl from inside. The tent flap fell away, and Leo caught a glimpse of pale arms reaching for the drunk, presumably Ricky. "Shit, what the hell," she exclaimed and smelled the vomit.

'It's okay, I just need sleep, it's okay,' mumbled Ricky, pushed himself past her and collapsed on the tent floor. Leo crouched down to the entrance.

"Hello," he shouted, "I am Leo. I am Leo. I accompanied him from the pump. Ricky waved one arm in Leo's direction.

He saved me, babe, we owe him.

'Oh! Thanks,' said Katie, giving him a quick smile before turning back to Ricky. Leo got an impression of big, innocent eyes and friendly features the second she faced him. It was hard to look at her properly in this light, but she seemed to be petite. Katie bent over to knock Ricky down and Leo caught a glimpse of a perfect peach-colored butt.

'Hey, let me help you,' said Leo and crawled into the tent. Together, they laid Ricky on the front and put a bowl under his mouth. Almost as soon as they sat down, Ricky started snoring.

Any excuse,' Katie said with a sinister look.

Happens a lot, doesn't it?

Every other week, always the same. "The way he grew up," Katie flicked angrily at a mud wrench. He said he'd change once we got married, but who knows when that will be.

"Wow, you are...

-Committed, yeah. Katie reached out a hand, the glimmer of a ring just visible. "He's wonderfully sober, but that's just...

"Too much?" Leo offered.

"Too much?" offered Leo. There was a brief pause. "So, are you camping around here?" Katie said.

'I have no idea,' Leo replied laughing. Red Zone, wherever that is.

'Oh shit', Katie replied, moving away from him and opening a map. 'Yes, it's about an hour's walk from here'.

'Seriously?' replied Katie. Leo looked over at the map. He had been walking in the opposite direction since the set was over.

"Urgh. He raised his hands in desperation.

'Oh, sorry,' said Katie and gave him a quick hug. You did a good thing tonight, fate will make it up to you. Leo felt her breasts pressing against him. As they parted, he carefully weighed his words.

I'm really tired and don't want to go back. So can I sleep here tonight?

"Uh..." he could feel that Katie was torn. Sure, why not? I guess we owe you one,' she said and showed him another smile.

She closed the tent and made room for him on the mattress by wrapping her sleeping bag around her. They lay there for a minute before Leo mentioned the obvious and asked her to share it with him. It was only a small sleeping bag, so they were squeezed together at the end, her hair in his face and her bottom against his crotch.

Time dragged on, and it was clear that neither of them were asleep. Leo turned the situation in his head and made his move. An arm around her stomach, ready to be pulled away when she said something. Not a word. He moved his hand to her chest, gently grabbed a handful and let it slide free. He felt her ass bump against him and she sighed.

They continued as it felt, forever, the question and the answer were obvious to both. One hand gradually became two and her top fell off. Katie had been rubbing against his erection the whole time, and when Leo's hand finally passed her panties, he noticed it was dripping.

His fingers slipped in gently, and the slightest caress of her clitoris left her breathless. Leo teased both her clitoris and her pussy, brought her close to orgasm and disappeared just before. He wanted her to be as horny as he could make her.

At the climax of a near orgasm, he pulled his pants down to her knees and maneuvered his cock between her legs. He slid up behind her and enjoyed the wetness of her cheating pussy.

Suddenly her hand grabbed his head and pulled him towards her. She kissed him hard on the cheek and whispered in his ear.

"I want you to cum inside me.

Leo fucked her slowly, with a little more force at the end of each stroke. It was for her, but also to prolong it. It was a raw thrill to fuck someone's fiancee while she was passed out next to you. It took everything he had not to fill her up right away.

He played for time, changed his position and rolled her over. Every stroke pushed her into the mattress. Out of an impulse, he wiggled his hand under her and reached for her chest, pressing her almost painfully.

His thrusts became fast but steady and he squeezed again. Katie gasped in time and Leo felt her pussy cramping up. He managed one more push, then a hard one came. His balls pumped to the rhythm of her pussy as he flowed in towards her. Both had tried hard to come quietly and it seemed to be enough. Ricky's snoring continued.

As they put their clothes back on, Leo smiled at the thought of his sperm warm inside her. Then he saw Katie leaning over Ricky and whispering something to his sleeping body. Leo thought Ricky was awake for a second, but he was definitely asleep. That's weird.

"What was that?" he whispered. Katie turned to Leo, and her face was surprisingly serious.

I said, "This is for you.

For the rest of the festival, they were a group. Katie was friendly but never flirted while Ricky was awake, picking up one load after another of Leo's sperm as Ricky fainted.

After each night, she whispered the same thing to Ricky, "This is for you.

Three months after the festival, Leo was surprised and happy to be invited to their wedding. It seemed as if something had pushed Ricky to turn the corner. Leo thought of his sperm seeping out of Katie on the last night of the festival and smiled as he clicked on "Present".

THE CABIN

I know how I got here; I just don't know what to do about it. Many of you will think I am a disgusting bitch who doesn't care about herself or others, and to tell you the truth, you are right. If you'd met me two years ago, you'd think I was a prude. You'd never believe that I've had sex with more than 10 different men in the last month. I don't even know most of their names. Still, I crave it. That's how it all started.

To tell you a little bit about me: I'm a small, fit redhead blessed (or sometimes cursed) with firm D-cup breasts. You tend to pay a lot of attention to me. At the same time I often wear clothes that play down their importance. I am a very active person, my husband calls me the Energizer Bunny. I do not go out often and we tend not to talk. Our circle of close friends is small. I work in the financial sector. My job is very demanding and stressful, but I am very well compensated. I guess other people would describe me as classy but friendly. Only recently I have developed a preference for quickies. My husband is more than willing to help me whenever I want. I had started to masturbate, sometimes with toys, when he was away on business.

We have two grown boys who don't live with us. One is in college, the other is working in the world of work. My husband is a good-looking man with a great job. We have a big house in the country. We love camping, going to concerts and doing all the normal things that people do.

There's one thing most people would never believe about me. I love sex, with strangers, outside. How I got to be like this is a pretty long story. Some people like the details, some people don't. I'm the former. This story will be detailed and you will understand how I felt at every step of this experience.

As I said before, I am active. I love a good run in the morning and often find myself hiking or kayaking, anything that takes me outside and into nature. I have always been like this. Last year, during my lunch break from work, I did some hiking on trails that are about 5 minutes away from my work by car. It is a kind of nature reserve, no vehicles are allowed. I drive there, put on my hiking boots and go for a little hike. The parking lot is not very big and there are rarely other cars there. Sometimes, when my husband is away on business, I drive there in the evening. We live in a small town and it is very safe.

The road system is quite complicated. In winter it is used as a cross-country skiing track, and in summer people go by bike, walk their dogs and hike there. The tracks have a fairly large outer loop, with quite a lot of forks and inner loops. I had taken the same route because I need just enough time to get around during my lunch break. On one occasion, last year, I decided to take another fork and follow one of the inner loops. I came across a small clearing and found a hut that is obviously used by skiers in winter. I got curious and went inside.

What I saw in the hut shocked me at first. There were indications that people had sex there. I found used condoms, wrappers etc. and even a pair of ladies' panties. At first I was quite disgusted and left. I thought, "What kind of slut would have sex in there and leave her panties behind? The next few days I started thinking about who would have sex in there. It seemed to me that it would most likely be people, probably married people, who would go there to cheat on their spouses. I told one of my long-time girlfriends what I had found in the woods and she told me that she and her current boyfriend were out there "grim". I'm not very familiar with the deviant sex vocabulary, so I had to get her to explain what she meant. Most of you know what it means, but she told me that her boyfriend loved going out into the woods with her and having sex there, sometimes in front of other people. I had no idea that was "a thing." I just couldn't figure out what kind of payoff it was for her, but she said it was very exciting and they didn't do it often.

In the following weeks I still hiked there, but avoided the hut. Apart from that I am a very curious woman and the train to the hut was always present. Every time I hiked, I found myself thinking about going back to the hut, not knowing exactly why, but it definitely occurred to me. I remember having the opportunity for an early lunch on a Wednesday and deciding to hike again. When I arrived at the parking lot, I noticed a very shiny new Lexus parked there. I ventured down the path. When I reached the fork in the road leading to the hut, the bait was too big; my curiosity forced me to do so. When I approached it, it seemed deserted. When I entered, I was shocked, repulsed and yet petrified. There was a middle-aged man, tall, obese, well-dressed. His fly was open and he was masturbating. I froze. Every fibre in my being told me to get out, but I couldn't move. He didn't stop, he just smiled at me and went on.

I still remember his look and his cock. He was focused on what he was doing, beads of sweat on his forehead. His cock was thick and long. His fleshy hands wrapped around it as he pumped it. He muttered a few words and persuaded me to "help". I shook my head negatively, but stayed there, feet away from him. He said something like, "Suit yourself, I don't mind if you watch." He went on for a few moments and then emitted a deep groan as huge streams of semen erupted from him. They flew so far that I had to lift my foot so he wouldn't splash it. He silently closed the zipper and slid past me on his way out. I was still in shock when I looked at his sperm on the floor. I couldn't believe how much it was.

When I came out of my stupor, I realized where I was and I was afraid of getting caught. I rushed out of the booth and back to my car. I returned to work and had 20 minutes left for lunch. Once there, I had calmed down sufficiently and realized that I was highly excited. I was so wet that I was afraid that employees and customers might recognize my state of arousal, so I made a decision as a manager. I went down the stairs to the floor below my office, found the handicapped washroom, went inside, locked the door and masturbated until orgasm. I came so hard that I was surprised that nobody heard me. Not only did I rub myself, but I put several fingers inside me and squirted quite a lot, so much that I had to clean the toilet I was sitting on.

I went back to my office and was quite ashamed, but I could NOT get the image of him masturbating out of my head. Luckily my husband was away on business, so I didn't have to worry about him feeling anything else about me. After work I got into my car. It was like a dream, I was in a haze, and when

I came to, I realized that I was in the parking lot of the hiking trails. I was trembling, excited and felt a little sick. Nevertheless, I got out of the car and walked down the paths towards the hut. To this day I don't know what I expected, but I found myself in the hut, sitting on the bench with my fingers in my pussy. I came, hard, and made up my panties and skirt. When I calmed down, I left the cabin. When I arrived at the beginning of the path, I saw a young couple with a blanket under their arms entering the path. I was horrified that they could see the wet stains on my skirt.

I got into my car and drove home. I was confused and frightened. I wondered what would have happened if I had been caught there. I fell asleep. The next morning I woke up and got ready for work. I thought about what kind of clothes I would have to wear to reduce the risk of my clothes being smeared with LOL. The only thing I could think of was to take a towel or blanket and when I went back, take off my underpants/panties and put them back on again. It was as if my subconscious had taken over, and when I wanted to leave I threw a small towel in the back of the car. When I got to work, I got my laptop and lunch from the back seat. I saw the towel I had put there and felt a little shame and disgust, but I quickly let that go out of my head.

This morning at work was LONG. I was restless and fidgety. I tried not to think about the cabin, but it kept popping into my mind. At lunch it was as if I was on autopilot. I found myself back in the cabin, naked from the waist down, sitting on my towel and fingered myself like crazy to get out as quickly as possible. Every little rustle that the wind made scared me, but finally I reached orgasm and hurried back to work. This routine lasted for several weeks until one day I was near my orgasm and a dog stuck his head in the cabin. I didn't hear him approaching and that really scared me. He didn't come into the cabin, his owner, a male dog, called him over and he ran away. My orgasm hit so violently that I literally splashed across the whole width of the room. I was so startled that I did not go back into the cabin for a few weeks.

In those few weeks my head was buzzing. Every time I was alone, I masturbated thinking about what would have happened if I had been caught. I had no preconceived ideas about what I would do, only the image of a stranger coming in the doorway while I was in the middle of orgasm made me cum hard. I squirted a lot and had masturbated on the floor of the washroom or in the bathtub to make it easier to clean up afterwards.

When I finally had the courage to return to the cabin, the season was almost over. I went there almost daily until it got too cold. It took longer and longer until I reached orgasm. I am now convinced that I deliberately slowed down to increase the chance that someone else would come in with me. That winter, I even convinced my husband to start cross-country skiing. We went to the hut a few times and even had a quickie there. The hut had been cleaned up by the skiers, the graffiti had been painted over and the floors had been well cleaned. Someone even installed a small wood stove on a big brick block outside, and more than once we found the hut to warm up.

Spring could not have come earlier for me. I seemed too anxious to return to the hut. The first hike did not go well. It was wet and muddy, and I turned back before I got there. I waited another week and masturbated at every opportunity. When I got back, it was dry enough to make it there. I masturbated slowly; I barely made it back to work in time. This routine continued for about a week. I still remember the day the routine changed. It was a Thursday, I had masturbated there at noon, and since my husband was not there, I went back in the evening. I got out of my car, grabbed my towel and headed for the hiking trail. When I entered the path, I looked back and saw another car entering the parking lot. A man got out. My heart was racing. He was alone. I noticed he was tall and thin, but I couldn't see him clearly. He definitely saw me, and as I walked along the path, he followed me, but kept his distance. I was wearing yoga pants, a tank top and a sweater.

When I came to the fork in the path leading to the cabin, my mind screamed that I should swerve, but my body had other ideas. I walked along the path. When I got to the cabin, I didn't know if he was still following me. I sat down on the bench and waited. My heart was racing. I didn't dare touch myself, although I was overexcited. In fact, I could hear him approaching. He stopped before he entered. I was paralyzed with fear. I was breathing very heavily. When he finally entered the cabin, he was about three feet in front of me. We didn't say anything, just stared at each other. Finally, I took the strength to ask him, "What do you want?" He answered, "I don't know," and he walked a few steps towards me. He was wearing nylon running trousers, including a sweatshirt and a muscle shirt. I looked at him, and he adjusted his stride. To this day I don't know what got into me, but I reached out my hand and felt his step. He was semi-erect and wasn't wearing any underpants.

Again it was like a dream. I stroked him a few times, then I rolled my fingers under the elastic waistband and pulled on him. His cock jumped free and then he was in my mouth. I sucked it eagerly. It wasn't huge, I had no problem taking the whole length. When he was about to cum, I thought about what I wanted to do, take him out and jerk him off? No, too risky, he might jerk off on me. He tried to pull away, but I held him there as his sperm shot out of his cock. I swallowed it. I remember thinking it wasn't as bad as I thought it was gonna be, swallowing. It tasted salty, earthy. When he pulled away from me, he pulled up his pants in silence and left. No thanks, it was good or something. He just walked away. I sat there, vibrating, ashamed and at the same time extremely aroused. I thought about leaving, but I didn't want to run into him again on the paths. I decided to drop myself off.

I took off my yoga pants and sat down on the bench again. It felt cold, but I started to touch myself. The mixed emotions stirred up my desire and soon I was completely gone. I realized that I was not determined to have a quick orgasm. I played with my lips and clitoris and enjoyed the sensations. Then I heard another sound. I froze. It sounded as if someone was approaching again. I sat there, half-naked on the bench, legs spread, hand on my sex, and my mind was moving at a million miles a minute. It felt like an eternity. I tormented myself putting my pants back on, but for some reason I didn't. When he entered the cabin, I immediately recognized him as the man I had walked into the season before. He smiled confidently and without a word, pulled his cock out. Before I knew it, I had his thick flesh in my hand and was stroking him. All I could think of was: "Holy shit, what am I doing, I just cheated on my husband with a complete stranger and now it's going to happen again".

I put it in my mouth. It tasted like sweat, very revolting, but I kept sucking. It erected in my mouth and it was too much for me. I gagged him, mainly because of the size, but partly also because of the smell. I felt sick to my stomach, but I kept on sucking. I just wanted to get rid of him and get out of there. He had other ideas. He seemed a little frustrated with my attempts to stick him in the throat. I gagged a lot. Eventually, he pulled it out of my mouth. He raised his hand in front of me and took out a condom. Almost robotically I took it off him, opened it and pushed it on him. He lifted me into a standing position and then told me to turn around. I hesitated and he took my elbow and led me. He is a whole lot bigger than me, so I knelt down on the bench voluntarily and I felt him touching my pussy. It was like electricity shooting through me. He pushed it against my hole. He adjusted my position and pushed it into me. My body literally exploded in orgasm.

He fucked me hard, holding me up with one arm around my waist. It was animalistic, and I was having orgasms all the time. He fucked me like a dog in heat. I could see he was about to orgasm, but he pulled the condom out and took it off. I was terribly afraid that he had put it back in me, but again he led me and turned me around and put the condom back in my face, twitching. Before I could react, he erupted in my face. His sperm was hot and thick and some of it ended up in my mouth, most of it was on my face and some of it ended up on my shirt and sweater. I realized that I was on my knees in front of him. I grabbed my towel and tried to clean up. At that point the light was very dim. He said a few words to me; I could not say which ones they were.

He closed the zipper and left. I sat down on the bench again and sobbed. Not only had I been very sloppy, but it was the first time I had cheated on my husband with two different men. I did not know their names. I cleaned up as much as I could. I put on my pants, but by then it was already dark. I left the cabin, and only when I came home did I realize that I had left my pants there. Now I was the bitch who fucks in the cabin.

Lightning Source UK Ltd.
Milton Keynes UK
UKHW022016190421
382278UK00003B/632